Oxford Progres
General Ed

M000187723

Jane Eyre

The *Oxford Progressive English Readers* series provides a wide range of reading for learners of English. It includes classics, the favourite stories of young readers, and also modern fiction. The series has five grades: the *Introductory Grade* at a 1400 word level, *Grade 1* at a 2100 word level, *Grade 2* at a 3100 word level, *Grade 3* at a 3700 word level and *Grade 4* which consists of abridged stories. Structural as well as lexical controls are applied at each level.

Wherever possible the mood and style of the original stories have been retained. Where this requires departure from the grading scheme, definitions and notes are given.

All the books in the series are attractively illustrated. Each book also has a short section containing questions and suggested activities for students.

Jane Eyre
Charlotte Brontë

Hong Kong
OXFORD UNIVERSITY PRESS
Oxford Singapore Tokyo

Oxford University Press

Oxford   New York   Toronto
Petaling Jaya   Singapore   Hong Kong   Tokyo
Delhi   Bombay   Calcutta   Madras   Karachi
Nairobi   Dar es Salaam   Cape Town
Melbourne   Auckland

and associated companies in
Berlin   Ibadan

© *Oxford University Press 1973*
First published 1973
Thirteenth impression 1988

OXFORD is a trade mark of Oxford University Press

Retold by Muriel Fyfe
Illustrated by Frank Po
Simplified according to the language grading scheme
especially compiled by D.H. Howe

ISBN 0 19 638257 2

Printed in Hong Kong by Liang Yu Printing Factory Ltd.
Published by Oxford University Press, Warwick House, Hong Kong

Contents

Contents

1 Gateshead

My name is Jane Eyre. My father was a poor clergy-man.* When I was a baby my father and mother died. I was left alone. I had no money and no friends.

My mother's brother, Uncle Reed, heard of my parents' death. He came soon after that to take me to stay 5 with him. He lived with his wife and three children in a large house called Gateshead. Uncle Reed was very kind to me. After a while my Uncle Reed, too, died. My aunt and my cousins did not like me. They were very cruel to me. The cruellest of them all was John, the 10 eldest.

John was a schoolboy. He was fat and big and he was fourteen years old. I was only ten and very small.

One day John and I had a fight. He hit me because I read some of his books. When his mother heard us 15 shouting she shouted angrily, 'Lock her in the Red Room.'

I was locked in a room which was dark and cold. My uncle had died in that room. I was very frightened. I cried and banged at the door but nobody let me out. 20 My cruel aunt left me there till I fainted.*

My aunt then called a doctor. He was a kind man. When he heard that my parents were dead and that I was unhappy in Gateshead, he told my aunt that I should go to school. 25

A few weeks later, we had a visitor. He was a tall and dark man.

*clergyman, a man who works for the church.
*faint, unable to know what is happening; unable to stay awake.

Mr. Brocklehurst

'Mr. Brocklehurst, this is Jane Eyre,' my aunt said.

'Are you a good girl, Jane?' asked Mr. Brocklehurst, the visitor.

I did not say a word.

5 'She's bad and she tells lies,' said my aunt. 'Tell all the teachers so at Lowood.'

'What a terrible thing,' said Mr. Brocklehurst. 'I will tell Miss Temple, the Headmistress, about her. All the girls at Lowood School eat very plain food and wear 10 simple clothes, but they work very hard.'

'That is exactly what Jane needs,' said my aunt. 'I don't want her to come home for her holidays. Let her spend her holidays at Lowood.'

'I shall do that, Mrs. Reed. I shall also tell Miss 15 Temple that Jane Eyre will be coming soon,' said Mr. Brocklehurst.

Then he went away. I was very hurt and sad that my aunt should say that I told lies in front of a visitor.

'I do not tell lies. I hate you and John. You are bad 20 and cruel,' I said.

2 Lowood

I left Gateshead for Lowood one cold morning in January. I went in a coach.* The coach was drawn by horses. It took me one day to reach Lowood.

I arrived at Lowood at night. In the dark I could see a large house with many windows. There were lights on *5* in some of the windows. I was taken straight to see Miss Temple, the Headmistress. She spoke to me kindly. I liked her at once. After that I was taken to a large room by Miss Miller, a teacher.

In that room there were eighty girls sitting at four *10* long tables. There were candles on the tables. The girls were doing their homework. They were not of the same age. Some were as young as nine while others were as old as twenty. They all wore old-fashioned brown dresses with pinafores* over them. Miss Miller asked me *15* to sit on a long seat near a door.

Then Miss Miller called, 'Monitors,* collect the lesson books!'

A tall girl from each table got up and put away the books. *20*

A poor supper

'Monitors, fetch the supper trays!'* called Miss Miller again.

*coach, a vehicle, with four wheels and usually pulled by horses, to carry people from one place to another.
*pinafore, a simple covering worn over a dress to keep it clean.
*monitor, headgirl of a class or classes.
*tray, flat piece of wood or metal on which to carry light things.

The tall girls went out and came back with our supper trays. They handed the trays round. On each tray there was only a small piece of cake and a cup of water. I could not eat because I was too tired but I drank a little
5   of the water.

After supper we said our prayers. Then we went to bed.

The bedroom was a long room with beds on each side facing each other. The beds were put very close together.
10   Two girls had to sleep on one bed. I had to share a bed with Miss Miller for that night. As I was very tired I soon fell asleep.

We got up very early the next morning. We said our prayers first. Then we had a Bible lesson before break-
15   fast. We had terrible food for breakfast. I could not eat it even though I was hungry.

I was not very happy at Lowood because most of the time I was cold and I did not get enough to eat.

3 Mr. Brocklehurst Visits Lowood

One day Mr. Brocklehurst came. He made me stand on a stool in front of all the girls and the teachers. He told them lies about me. He told them how kind my aunt was. He also told them not to talk to me and he made me stand there on the stool for half an hour.　　　　　5

When Mr. Brocklehurst went away, all the girls went to tea. I got down and cried. Just then someone came. It was an older girl called Helen Burns. She was very friendly. She brought me my tea and talked to me kindly.　　　　　10

Then Miss Temple came and took us to her room. It was a warm room. I felt happy there. Miss Temple gave us tea.

I told her about Gateshead and my Aunt Reed. I told her about the kind doctor at Gateshead. She believed 15 me. She said that she would write to the doctor to ask him about me.

A week later she received a letter from the kind doctor. She then told everyone at Lowood that what Mr. Brocklehurst said about me was not true.　　　　　20

Everybody was pleased to hear that. That made me very, very happy. From then on I liked Miss Temple even more.

4 Helen Burns

Spring came after the cold winter. The sunshine was warm and lovely, but Lowood was not a healthy place. It was too wet.

In May most of the girls were ill with fever. Some
5 went home, but some were too ill to be moved. Those who were not ill were allowed to play outside by the river because the teachers were too busy looking after the sick.

While playing outdoors I often wished that Helen was
10 with me but Helen was very ill.

One night I went very quietly to see her. I did not want to wake anyone up because no one was allowed to see her.

She was in Miss Temple's room, but Miss Temple was
15 not there.

'Helen,' I called her softly.

She heard me. She was very weak and thin.

'Have you come to say good-bye?' she said. I knew she was going to die. I tried very hard not to cry.

20 'Don't leave me, Jane,' she said. So I climbed into bed with her and soon we fell asleep. Next morning she was dead.

5 A New Job

I was at Lowood for eight years. I later became a teacher. All through my stay at Lowood, Miss Temple was my friend as well as my teacher. She taught me and helped me a lot. I was very happy while she was there.

At the end of my second year as a teacher, Miss Temple got married to a clergyman. When she left Lowood I was very sad. I wanted to leave too. I wanted to find a new job. 5

I put an advertisement* in the newspaper. A week later I got a reply. It said: 10

'A teacher is needed to teach a little girl about ten years old. The salary is £30 a year. Please send name, address and general information to Mrs. Fairfax, Thornfield, North Millcote.'

£30 a year seemed a lot of money to me. At Lowood I was only getting £15 a year. 15

I left Lowood two weeks later with very few things.

*advertisement, a notice in a newspaper about a job or product.

6 Thornfield Hall

Thornfield was six miles from Millcote. A servant put the box holding my belongings on top of a small carriage* at Millcote and he drove very slowly towards Thornfield. It was dark when I reached Thornfield Hall.

5   I was taken into a small warm room where a little old lady sat knitting. She had on a black silk dress with a pretty white apron* over it. She got up.

'How do you do, my dear?' she said.

She invited me to have supper with her. After supper
10   I said, 'Where's Miss Fairfax?'

'You mean Adele Varens? She's not my daughter. I have no family. I'm glad you have come. It is lonely here for me.'

Later she took me up to my room. It was warm and
15   neat. It had pretty blue curtains and wallpaper, so unlike Lowood with its dirty and empty walls. I thanked God that night before I slept.

Next morning I got up very early. I went out to look at the garden. It was a pretty garden and the house was
20   very large.

Mrs. Fairfax came out too. I learned from her that the owner was a Mr. Rochester, and Adele Varens, my pupil, was his ward.* She also told me that Adele was

*carriage, a vehicle on four wheels and pulled by horses for carrying people. It is smaller than a coach.
*apron, a loose covering tied over the front of clothes to keep them clean.
*ward, a young person under the care of someone who is not the parent.

born in France and that her mother died only six
months ago.

A strange noise

Just then Adele, a thin little girl of about eight, came
rushing towards us. Her nurse was with her. They both
spoke in French. Mrs. Fairfax introduced us. I spoke to 5
her in French. Adele was glad to find that I could speak
French too.

We had our first lesson that day. After that Mrs. Fairfax showed me round the house. There were many large
rooms filled with rich furniture. We even went right to 10
the top part of the house which had no roof. From
there we could see the fields far away.

The top floor of the house was quite dark and the
doors of the rooms were all shut. Only one light shone
from a small window at one end. 15

Suddenly I heard a strange noise. It stopped and then
it started again.

'Mrs. Fairfax, what's that?' I asked.

'Maybe it's Grace Poole, a servant,' she said. Then she
called, 'Grace!' 20

A huge woman came out from a door near me. She
did not look a kind woman. Mrs. Fairfax told Grace that
there was too much noise. Grace then went quietly back
into the room.

7 Mr. Rochester

Winter had come. The ground was covered with ice. It was very cold.

One afternoon I wanted to post a letter at the village. The village was only two miles away. I walked for a
5 while. Feeling tired I sat down beside the road to rest.

I saw a man on a horse coming towards me. There was a dog too. It was big and black. The man was broad but not tall. He had a dark and sad face. I guessed he must be about thirty-five years old.

10 He passed me with his dog. Suddenly the horse slipped on the ice and the man fell with the horse. The dog began to bark as though asking for help. I went there as quickly as I could for the ground was slippery.

He got up just as I reached him. 'Are you hurt?' I
15 asked him.

The master of Thornfield Hall returns

'Thank you, I am not hurt,' he said. 'Where do you live?'

'I live at Thornfield Hall,' I said. 'I am the governess* there.'

20 He tried to stand up but found it too painful. 'Please help me to my horse,' he said.

I helped him.

'Thank you,' he said and rode away.

When I reached Thornfield Hall after posting my
25 letter it was getting dark. I was glad to be inside because it was bright and warm. I could hear happy voices, es-

*governess, a woman who looks after and teaches a child in the child's home.

pecially Adele's, but when I walked into the room I saw
only the big black dog lying beside the fire.

'Whose dog is that?' I asked the maid.

'It's Mr. Rochester's. The master is home. He's with
the doctor. He hurt himself,' said the maid.   5

Adele was too excited to do her lessons properly. She
was happy too. Mrs. Fairfax told me later that we had
been asked to have tea with Mr. Rochester at six
o'clock.

When tea-time came I went into the drawing room. I   10
had on my black silk dress. In the room was a man
sitting on a couch* with one foot stretched out on a
cushion. Mrs. Fairfax, Adele and the dog were there too.
The man on the couch was none other than the man I
met yesterday. That was Mr. Rochester, the master of   15
Thornfield Hall.

He was not very friendly. He did not say anything
about the accident.

Mr. Rochester speaks to me

We had tea. After that he told me to sit by the fire.
He told me that he was pleased that Adele had learnt   20
quite a lot in three months.

'Where did you come from?' he asked.

'Lowood School,' I answered.

'How long were you there?' he said.

'Eight years,' I said.   25

He then asked me to play the piano. I played. I only
stopped when he told me to. He liked my playing.

He wanted to see some drawings of mine which Adele
showed him. I showed him more.

Suddenly he stopped and wished us good night. He   30
was a very strange man. I thought he was quite rude.

*couch, a long, comfortable piece of furniture for sitting or lying on.

After putting Adele to bed I went to see Mrs. Fairfax
in her room. She told me that Mr. Rochester did not say
much and seemed rude because he had a lot of worries.

'He does not like Thornfield Hall. He does not often
5 stay here for more than two weeks,' said Mrs. Fairfax.

But Mr. Rochester stayed longer this time. He became more friendly. I grew to like him.

8   The Fire

One night I was asleep in bed when a strange sound
woke me up. It was a frightening sound. My room was
dark. I sat up listening. There was not a sound. I tried to
sleep again. Suddenly I heard a noise at my door.

'Who's there?' I called out.   5

No one answered. I became very frightened. Then I
heard a sound like wicked laughter near my door. Next
moment I heard the steps of someone running. A door
banged after that.

I got up to look for Mrs. Fairfax, but when I opened   10
my door, I saw smoke. It came out from Mr. Rochester's room.

I ran into my master's room. He was asleep on his bed
and his bed was on fire.

'Wake up, wake up,' I cried.   15

I poured some water on the burning bedclothes. He
woke up. When he got up I told him what happened.
He told me to sit down. Then, he went out holding a
candle. I sat in the darkness to wait. He came back after
a long time.   20

'It was Grace Poole. Go back to sleep now. Don't say
anything to anyone. I shall tell them myself.'

'Good night, sir,' I said.

'Good night, Jane. Thank you for saving my life to-
night,' said my master.   25

I went back to my room.

Next morning I found Grace Poole sewing rings onto
some new curtains. She told me that they were for my
master's room.

9 Mr. Mason

Mr. Rochester went away for two weeks after the fire. He came back with some friends. One of them was a beautiful and rich young woman called Miss Blanche Ingram. My master spent a lot of time with her. I did not like her.   5

One evening we had a visitor. His name was Mr. Mason. When I told Mr. Rochester about Mr. Mason, he looked worried and ill. Then they both went into the library.

In the middle of that night, I woke up because the moon was very bright. Suddenly I heard someone crying   10
out in pain. Someone shouted, 'Help me! Help me! Rochester!'

There was a lot of noise. Then all was quiet. Everyone asked, 'What happened? Is anyone hurt?' Mr. Rochester   15
came down to where we were. 'Everything's fine. It was only a servant having a bad dream,' he said.

The guests all went back to their rooms. I too went back to my room. I could not sleep. I sat thinking of what had happened. A little later, when everything was   20
quiet, Mr. Rochester came to ask for my help.

Mr. Mason is hurt

We went to a room on the next floor. In this room there was an open door behind a curtain. I could hear something like animal noises coming from the room behind the curtain. I thought it was Grace Poole.   25

Mr. Rochester shut the door quickly. There I saw a man sitting on a chair. Mr. Rochester and I went near.

I was surprised to find that it was Mr. Mason. He was hurt. One arm was covered with blood.

I cleaned the wound. Then Mr. Rochester went to get the doctor.

5 'What happened?' asked the doctor. 'This man looks as though he has been bitten.'

'She bit me after Mr. Rochester took the knife away,' said Mr. Mason weakly.

'I told you not to go near her alone,' Mr. Rochester
10 said. I did not understand what they were saying.

10   Mr. Rochester Asks Me to Be His Wife

The next day Mr. Mason was gone.

I told Mr. Rochester that my Aunt Reed of Gateshead wanted to see me.

'Why do you have to go, Jane?' asked my master.

'Mrs. Reed has asked for me, sir. She's dying. I won't   5
be away long. I shall come back as soon as I can,' I said.

Before my aunt died she told me that my father's brother wrote to ask about me three years ago. He wrote from Madeira. He wanted me to live with him and be his daughter.   10

'I told him you died at Lowood,' said my aunt.

She still hated me. I stayed on for a while at Gateshead.

One day I received a letter from Mrs. Fairfax. She told me that Mr. Rochester had gone to London. She   15
wrote that he might have gone to arrange his wedding to Miss Ingram.

When I read Mrs. Fairfax's letter I was very sad. I did not want Mr. Rochester to marry Miss Ingram.

I return to Thornfield Hall

I returned to Millcote without Mrs. Fairfax knowing.   20
I walked from Millcote to Thornfield Hall. I met Mr. Rochester sitting by the road not far from Thornfield Hall. He seemed glad to see me. I was very happy to see him again.

At Thornfield Hall Mrs. Fairfax and Adele were   25
happy that I was back. Mr. Rochester spent a lot of his

time with Adele and me. I was glad. I felt that I loved my master.

One warm evening, I met Mr. Rochester in the garden. He was looking at the pretty flowers. We talked about his marriage. We also talked about the time for me to leave Thornfield Hall. I felt so sad that I started to cry.

'Why do you cry?' he asked.

'Because I have to leave. I love everyone here,' I cried.

'Why do you leave then?' said Mr. Rochester.

I agree to marry Mr. Rochester

'You are marrying Miss Ingram. You don't need a governess any more,' I said.

'I don't want to marry Miss Ingram. I don't love her. I want to marry you, Jane. Will you be my wife?' Mr. Rochester said gently.

Suddenly I felt so happy that I wanted to shout and sing.

'Sir, if you truly love me, I will gladly be your wife,' I said.

Next morning Mr. Rochester told Mrs. Fairfax of our plans for the wedding. Mrs. Fairfax was not very happy though.

'I wish you well, Jane. But do take care. I hope that everything will be all right for you,' said Mrs. Fairfax.

I was surprised to hear Mrs. Fairfax speaking in such a strange way.

11   A Visitor in My Room

Mr. Rochester bought me a lot of presents. He bought dresses and jewels.

I too wanted to give him presents, but I had no money. Then I remembered my uncle in Madeira who wanted me to live with him. I wrote and told him that   *5* I was alive. I told him that I would be marrying Mr. Rochester of Thornfield Hall in a month's time.

During the month I got everything ready. My clothes were packed. We would spend our honeymoon in London. Then I would be Jane Rochester instead of Jane   *10* Eyre.

Two days before the wedding I opened the box with my wedding dress in it. I took out my wedding dress. It was made of grey silk. It looked beautiful to me. In the box there was also a lovely veil* made of lace. It was   *15* a present from Mr. Rochester.

I wanted to thank Mr. Rochester very much but he was away in London. I hung my wedding dress and the veil in the wardrobe* before I went to bed that night.

It was late, but I could not sleep. The wind blew   *20* loud and strong outside. When I finally fell asleep, I had two bad dreams.

The first one was about Mr. Rochester riding away from Thornfield Hall. I tried to call him back, but he did not hear me.   *25*

The second dream was about Thornfield Hall. I

*veil, something made of thin and soft material that women use to
    cover their heads with.
*wardrobe, a cupboard for hanging up clothes.

dreamed that it was destroyed. In the
dream I stood on a broken wall and
watched Mr. Rochester riding away. Suddenly I fell. Then I woke up.

The woman in my room

5   I saw a lighted candle on the dressing
table. My wardrobe door was open. I
heard someone moving about, but I could
not see anyone. Thinking it was Sophie, the
maid, I called out, 'What are you doing,
10 Sophie?'

    No one answered. Then I saw someone
take the candle and walk towards the wardrobe. It was a woman. She looked at my
wedding dress. Then she held the light up.
15 I saw her but she was not Sophie nor Grace

Poole nor Mrs. Fairfax. She was a large woman in a white dress. As I looked at her, she put the candle down. She put my veil on her head. I could see her face in the mirror then. Her face was frightening and swollen. Her
5 eyes were red and her lips were purple. Her hair was long and uncombed. I was too frightened to scream.

She looked at herself for a while in the mirror. Then she pulled off the veil. She tore it in two, threw it on the floor and stepped on it.
10 On her way out she stopped by my bed. She looked at me with those terrible red eyes. Then I fainted.

Mr. Rochester came home the next day. I told him of my dream. He just laughed and told me not to worry.

Then I told him of the woman with the red eyes.
15 'It must have been another dream. You are too excited over the wedding,' said Mr. Rochester.

'But I found the veil, torn in two, on the floor,' I said.

He looked worried.

'Thank God nothing happened to you,' he said.

12 The Wedding Day

On the day of my wedding, I got up early. Sophie helped me put on my wedding dress and the plain veil.

Mr. Rochester walked me to the church. We did not invite anyone. As we arrived at the church, I saw two strange men walking in the graveyard.* When they saw us they went to the back of the church. 5

We then walked into the church. The clergyman was waiting at the altar.* We walked towards the altar. The two strangers were standing at the back of the church. When we were ready the clergyman said, 'If either of you know any reason why these two may not be married, please say it now.' 10

'They cannot be married,' one of the men behind us said.

No one said a word for a while. 15

Mr. Rochester has a wife

'What is your reason?' asked the clergyman.

'Mr. Rochester has a wife,' said the stranger.

'Who are you?' asked Mr. Rochester.

'My name is Briggs. I am a lawyer from London. Fifteen years ago you married a Bertha Mason in Jamaica. I have the marriage papers.' 20

Then another man came forward. He was Mr. Mason who was hurt one night at Thornfield Hall. Mr. Rochester was very angry.

*graveyard, place behind a church, where dead people are buried.
*altar, a raised table or platform where priests perform religious acts and give praise to god.

'I saw my sister at Thornfield Hall in April,' said Mr. Mason.

Mr. Rochester kept quiet for a while. Then he said, 'What this man said is true. I have a wife. But she is mad. This girl beside me knew nothing about it. Please come with me to Thornfield Hall to see for yourself.'

Still holding my hand Mr. Rochester led us all, the clergyman, the lawyer and Mr. Mason to Thornfield Hall.

13   Mr. Rochester's Mad Wife

At Thornfield Hall, Mrs. Fairfax and Adele were waiting
for us with smiles on their faces. But before they could
say anything Mr. Rochester said angrily, 'Away with
your good wishes. We don't need them!'

He took me up to the third floor. He unlocked a door   5
and we went in.

'This is where she bit you. Do you remember, Mason?' said Mr. Rochester.

Mr. Mason did not answer.

Then Mr. Rochester unlocked the door behind the   10
curtain and we walked into a dark room. Grace Poole
was cooking near the fire. There was a wild-looking
person running about the room. She looked more like
an animal than a woman.

The mad woman

Mr. Rochester spoke then. When the wild-looking   15
woman heard the voice, she rushed towards him. She
was none other than the woman with red eyes who tore
my veil.

Suddenly she ran up to Mr. Rochester and tried to
bite him. Mr. Rochester struggled with her. Grace Poole   20
brought a rope and she and Mr. Rochester managed to
tie her to a chair. All that time she was screaming
loudly.

Mr. Rochester stood up and said, 'That's the wife I
have been married to for fifteen years.'   25

I was shocked and surprised. We all left the room except Mr. Rochester. On the way down the lawyer said,

'Mr. Mason will tell your uncle about this. Your uncle will not blame you for this.'

'Do you know my uncle?' I asked.

'He's very ill. He may not live long,' said the lawyer.

I decide to leave

5   When Mr. Mason and the lawyer had left, I went into my room. I was very sad and I did not know what to do. I prayed to God. Then I got the answer. I must leave Thornfield Hall.

Later when I came out, I found Mr. Rochester
10 waiting for me. We went into the library. He told me how his father tricked him into marrying Bertha Mason. She was rich but mad when Mr. Rochester married her. He then begged me to go away with him.

'I can't. It would be wrong,' I said.

15 'Please don't leave me, Jane. I love you. Come with me. We will go far away where no one will know us,' said Mr. Rochester.

I left him there on the sofa and I went up to my room. I had to leave him.

14 I Leave Thornfield Hall

I locked myself in my room till midnight. When everything was quiet, I took my clothes and some food. I put
all my money — twenty shillings — in my pocket. I crept
quietly out of the house feeling very sad.

I walked for some time across fields and woods until   5
I was too tired to walk. Then a coach came along and
I climbed on to the coach and asked the driver to take
me as far as he could for twenty shillings.

I had no more money, but I did not care. I just
wanted to go far away from Thornfield Hall.   10

Two days later, I reached a place called Whitcross.
The driver told me that was as far as he could take me
for twenty shillings. So I got down and watched the
coach go. After the coach had left, I found that I had   15
left my belongings in it. I had no food, no money and
no clothes. What was I to do?

That night I ate wild fruit and slept out in the open.

The next day I tried to look for work, but nobody
wanted me. I was tired, cold and hungry. I walked and
walked for another two days without any food. It was   20
raining too.

I ask for help

When night came I saw a light in the distance. I
walked slowly towards the light. I peeped through the
window and I saw a clean kitchen. There were three
women sitting in it. One was old. She was knitting. The   25
other two were young and they had kind faces. I could
hear them calling each other. Their names were Mary

and Diana. The older woman's name was Hannah. She
was a servant.

I knocked at the door and Hannah opened it.

'What do you want?' she asked.

5   'Please may I come in? I'm cold and hungry and I've
nowhere to go,' I said.

'You can't sleep here but you can have some bread,'
she said.

'Please don't send me away. Let me speak to your
10   mistresses,' I begged her.

But she told me to go away and she shut the door in
my face.

I was so tired that I just sat down where I was
standing.

I am given food and a bed

15   Just then a man came up. He looked at me and said
something to me. He knocked at the door. Hannah
opened the door.

'My, you are all wet. Come in quickly, Mr. St. John,'
said Hannah. Then she saw me.

20   'Go away. Don't sit here all night,' she said.

'Hush, Hannah,' St. John said, 'We must find out
what's wrong with her. Come into the house, young
woman.' He helped me into the nice warm kitchen.

'Who is it, brother?' one sister cried.

25   'I don't know. I found her outside the door in the
cold,' said St. John.

I sat down and Diana brought me some food. I ate
everything up quickly. After I had eaten, St. John
asked, 'What's your name?'

30   I thought for a while and I said, 'Jane Elliott.' I did
not want him to know my real name.

They asked me questions about myself and where I lived. I told them that I was too tired and weak to talk. So Hannah took me upstairs to a clean dry room. She helped me take my wet clothes off and put me to bed. 5 I fell asleep straight away.

For three days and nights I was ill. I stayed in bed all the time. Hannah looked after me. Sometimes Diana and Mary came to talk to me.

I explain who I am

After the third day, I felt better. So I got up and put 10 on my clothes which had been cleaned by Hannah. I went downstairs to the kitchen and talked to Hannah.

She told me that St. John, Diana and Mary were brother and sisters. She also told me that their name was Rivers and that the house was called Moor House. Their 15 father had just died.

'Misses Mary and Diana are both governesses in London and Mr. St. John is a clergyman. They are all here because they are on holiday,' said Hannah.

Then Diana and Mary came into the kitchen. When 20 they found me there they brought me into the sitting-room. St. John was reading in the sitting-room. He was tall and handsome. He had fair hair and blue eyes.

'Where's your home, Miss Elliott? Have you any friends? We can tell them you are here,' said St. John.

25 'I have no home and no friends,' I said. 'My father was a clergyman. He and my mother died when I was a child. I spent eight years at Lowood School. Before I came here I was a governess. I had to leave my work. Please don't ask me why. I can't tell you.'

30 'I won't question you further then,' said St. John.

'Thank you, sir. I want to thank all of you too for letting me stay here. I would have died if not for you, sir,' I said.

'We're glad to have you, Jane,' said the two sisters.

I then asked if they could help me find work.

St. John finds work for me

The Rivers family was very kind to me. Diana was very clever. She knew German so I asked her to teach me. Mary saw some of my drawings and she asked me to draw. Time passed happily enough for me there. I still thought a lot about Mr. Rochester.

One day St. John got a letter. 'Uncle John's dead,' he said.

Diana and Mary read the letter. They did not look sad.

'Jane, you must be wondering why we are not sad. You see, we've never seen Uncle John. He was my mother's brother. He quarrelled with our mother. Now he has left £20,000 to another relation,' said Diana.

St. John found me work as a school teacher in his parish.* I was paid £30 a year and I could stay at a cottage near the school. I was very thankful to St. John.

I had twenty pupils in my school. Most of them were difficult to teach. Three could read but none could write.

In the evenings I was very lonely in my cottage. I wished Mr. Rochester was there with me. I spent a lot of time drawing.

St. John came often to see me. One day he looked at my drawings. Then he tore off one corner of my drawing and put it into his glove. I thought it most strange, but I did not say anything.

My uncle leaves me a fortune

The next day St. John came again. He told me that

*parish, a district with its own church and clergyman.

Mr. Briggs, the lawyer, asked if he knew anyone called Jane Eyre. I was surprised. 'You are Jane Eyre, aren't you?' he asked. He showed the piece of paper he had torn from my drawing. It had 'Jane Eyre' written on
5 it.

'Yes, I am Jane Eyre. But why does Mr. Briggs want to know?' I asked.

'Well, your uncle, John Eyre, has died in Madeira and he has left you £20,000,' said St. John.
10 ' £20,000!' I said. I was too surprised to believe it.

'But how did you find out I was the one Mr. Briggs was looking for?' I asked.

'My mother's name was Eyre. She had two brothers. One of them was John Eyre. The other was a clergyman
15 who died a long time ago. He had a little girl called Jane Eyre,' said St. John.

I share my good fortune

'Why, that makes your mother my aunt then. And you, Diana and Mary are my cousins. Oh, how happy I am. Now I have relations of my own. I will share uncle's
20 money with all three of you,' I said happily.

St. John did not want me to share the money. But later he, Diana and Mary agreed after I begged them to.

We lived happily in Moor House together. Mary and Diana did not have to work in London any more.
25 St. John wanted to go to India to help the people there and to teach them about God. He asked me to go with him as his wife. I could not do that because I still loved Mr. Rochester.

One evening I suddenly thought I heard Mr. Roches-
30 ter calling me. His voice went on calling, 'Jane, Jane.'

I ran out into the garden but I could see no one. Then I knew I had to go back to Thornfield Hall.

15 Ferndean

The next day I left Moor House. I told Diana and Mary
I was going to see a friend that I was worried about.
They did not ask any questions.

I went by coach. After leaving my things at an inn,*
I walked to Thornfield Hall. I was happy and excited   5
when I reached the gate to Thornfield Hall. I looked
through the gate and I saw an old burnt house. It did
not look like the Thornfield Hall I knew. Some of the
walls had fallen down. There was no roof.

I went back to the inn. I asked the innkeeper who   10
had been a servant at Thornfield Hall years ago, what
had happened.

He told me this story.

'The house was burnt down eleven months ago. The
people said that it was Mr. Rochester's mad wife who
did it. Mr. Rochester found her on the roof in the   15
burning house. He went up to try to save her. But when
she saw him, she threw herself down from the roof.'

'How is Mr. Rochester?' I asked.

'The house fell on Mr. Rochester just as he was trying
to get out. He was rescued but he lost one hand in the   20
fire and he is also blind,' said the innkeeper.

'Where is he now?' I asked.

'He lives at Ferndean, about thirty miles from here.
He lives with Old John, the driver, and his wife,' the innkeeper said.   25

I then asked for a carriage to take me to see my poor
master. I paid the driver twice what he asked.

*inn, a place where travellers may eat, drink or even spend the night.

I go to Ferndean

Ferndean was old and not big like Thornfield Hall. There were no other houses around.

As I was walking towards the house, I saw my master coming out slowly. He stretched out his arms to help
5 him find the way. He looked so tired and sad.

Just then it started to rain. I saw John come out to help him into the house, but Mr. Rochester would not let him. He went in the same way he came out.

I walked to the door and knocked. John's wife, Mary,
10 opened the door. She was so surprised that she looked at me for a long time before she spoke. I told her that I had come to see my master.

She took me into the kitchen. John was there. I sat down by the fire while John went to fetch my luggage.
15 Then the sitting-room bell rang. Mary put a glass and two lighted candles on a tray.

'Give me the tray. I'll take it to him,' I said.

Mary opened the sitting-room door and I walked in. My hands shook. I was not sure if he wanted to see me
20 because Mary said earlier that he did not allow anyone into the sitting-room except John and herself.

Mr. Rochester thinks he is dreaming

The sitting-room was dark. Mr. Rochester was standing near the fireplace looking sad and tired. His old
25 black dog, Pilot, lay near him.

When Pilot saw me, he jumped at me and barked. He remembered me. Mr. Rochester thought I was Mary.

'Give me the water, Mary,' he said.

I gave him the glass of water.
30 Pilot was still jumping all over me, so I said, 'Down, Pilot.'

Mr. Rochester listened. Then he said, 'It's you, Mary, isn't it?'

'Mary's in the kitchen,' I said.

He put out his hand as though to touch me, but I was too far away.

'Who's there? Tell me,' he said.

'Pilot knows me,' I said while I held his hand. 'I'm Jane Eyre. I've come back. I'm never going to leave you again.'

He felt my hands, my dress and my face.

'Jane Eyre! It's you. Am I dreaming?' said Mr. Rochester.

'No. I'm Jane Eyre. You're not dreaming,' I said.

5 We sat down and I asked Mary to bring us supper. Mr. Rochester started asking me questions. I told him everything the next day.

16   We Are Married at Last

The next day we took a walk in the fields. I told him all that had happened to me. Mr. Rochester asked me a lot of questions. He told me how he had suffered.

'Marry me now, Jane. I am now old and blind. I have no money to buy jewels and fine clothes,' said Mr. Rochester. 5

I agreed to marry him. Then happily we walked back to the cottage.

Three days later I became Mrs. Rochester. I wrote to the Rivers. Diana and Mary wrote back to say how 10 happy they were, but St. John did not reply.

I went to see Adele, who was in a boarding-school.* She was unhappy there so I brought her home. Later I put her in another school where she was happy. I looked after Adele as though she was my real daughter. 15

One morning, two years later, Mr. Rochester came close to me and said, 'Jane, are you wearing a pale blue dress and have you something bright around your neck?'

'Yes,' I said. 'Can you see them?'

'Yes, I can see a little,' he said. 20

At once we went to London to see a doctor. The doctor treated Mr. Rochester. Soon he could see better with one eye. He could not see enough to read or write, but he could walk about the place without feeling about like a blind person. At least he could see the eyes and face 25 of our first child, a boy.

We have been married for over ten years now and we have been very, very happy.

*boarding-school, a school where children may also take meals and live.

Questions

Chapter 1	1. Where did Jane go after her parents died?
	2. Why did Jane fight with John?
	3. What was 'the Red Room'?
	4. What did pupils at Lowood do?
Chapter 2	1. Who was the headmistress of Lowood?
	2. How many girls stayed at Lowood?
	3. Say whether Jane was happy or unhappy at Lowood and give reasons for your answer.
Chapter 3	1. What did Mr. Brocklehurst make Jane do?
	2. Who was friendly to Jane?
	3. How did Miss Temple help Jane?
Chapter 4	1. What did Jane think of while playing outdoors?
	2. Why did Jane feel like crying when she visited Helen Burns?
Chapter 5	1. For how long did Jane stay at Lowood?
	2. Why did Jane want to leave Lowood at the end of her second year as a teacher there?
Chapter 6	1. Who greeted Jane on her arrival at Thornfield Hall?
	2. What was the name of Jane's pupil?
	3. In what ways was Thornfield Hall different from Lowood?
	4. Why was Adele at Thornfield Hall?

Chapter 7 1. Where was Jane going one afternoon in winter?
2. While Jane was resting, a man on a horse came towards her. Can you describe him?
3. Who had come to Thornfield Hall?
4. Did Jane like Mr. Rochester? Why?

Chapter 8 1. What woke Jane up one night?
2. Where did the smoke come from?
3. What was on fire?

Chapter 9 1. Was Mr. Rochester happy to see Mr. Mason?
2. Who was in the room behind the curtain?
3. What had happened to him?

Chapter 10 1. What did Aunt Reed say to Jane before she died?
2. Why was Jane sad when she read Mrs. Fairfax's letter?
3. What did Jane and Mr. Rochester talk about?
4. Why did Jane think she would have to leave Thornfield Hall?
5. Was Mrs. Fairfax happy when she was told of the wedding?

Chapter 11 1. Whom did Jane write to before her wedding?
2. Why couldn't Jane thank Mr. Rochester for his present?
3. What was Jane's second dream about?
4. Who was in Jane's room?

Chapter 12 1. Who were the two strange men at the wedding?
2. Why could Jane not marry Mr. Rochester?
3. Why did Mr. Rochester keep his wife a secret?

Chapter 13 1. Who were in the locked room on the third floor?
2. What did the wild-looking woman do when Mr. Rochester spoke?
3. Why did Mr. Rochester marry a mad woman?
4. What did Jane decide to do?

Chapter 14 1. Where did the coach take Jane?
2. Why was Jane without food and clothes?
3. Whose house did she reach after walking for two days?
4. St. John received a letter one day. What was it about?
5. How did St. John know that Jane was the person Mr. Briggs was looking for?
6. What did Jane do with the money left to her?

Chapter 15 1. What had become of Thornfield Hall?
2. What happened to Mr. Rochester during the fire?
3. How did Mr. Rochester's mad wife die?
4. Whom did Mr. Rochester live with at Ferndean?
5. Do you think Mr. Rochester was glad that Jane had returned?

Chapter 16 1. Why did St. John not reply to Jane's letter?
2. Where was Adele?
3. When was Mr. Rochester able to see again?

Oxford Progressive English Readers

Introductory Grade

Vocabulary restricted to 1400 headwords
Illustrated in full colour

The Call of the Wild and Other Stories	Jack London
Emma	Jane Austen
Jungle Book Stories	Rudyard Kipling
Life Without Katy and Seven Other Stories	O. Henry
Little Women	Louisa M. Alcott
The Lost Umbrella of Kim Chu	Eleanor Estes
Tales from the Arabian Nights	Retold by Rosemary Border
Treasure Island	R.L. Stevenson

Grade 1

Vocabulary restricted to 2100 headwords
Illustrated in full colour

The Adventures of Sherlock Holmes	Sir Arthur Conan Doyle
Alice's Adventures in Wonderland	Lewis Carroll
A Christmas Carol	Charles Dickens
The Dagger and Wings and Other Father Brown Stories	G.K. Chesterton
The Flying Heads and Other Strange Stories	Retold by C. Nancarrow
The Golden Touch and Other Stories	Retold by R. Border
Great Expectations	Charles Dickens
Gulliver's Travels	Jonathan Swift
Hijacked!	J.M. Marks
Jane Eyre	Charlotte Brontë
Lord Jim	Joseph Conrad
Oliver Twist	Charles Dickens
The Stone Junk	Retold by D.H. Howe
Stories of Shakespeare's Plays 1	Retold by N. Kates
Tales from Tolstoy	Retold by R.D. Binfield
The Talking Tree and Other Stories	David McRobbie
The Treasure of the Sierra Madre	B. Traven
True Grit	Charles Portis

Grade 2

Vocabulary restricted to 3100 headwords
Illustrated in colour

The Adventures of Tom Sawyer	Mark Twain
Alice's Adventures through the Looking Glass	Lewis Carroll
Around the World in Eighty Days	Jules Verne
Border Kidnap	J.M. Marks
David Copperfield	Charles Dickens
Five Tales	Oscar Wilde
Fog and Other Stories	Bill Lowe
Further Adventures of Sherlock Holmes	Sir Arthur Conan Doyle

Grade 2 (cont.)

The Hound of the Baskervilles	Sir Arthur Conan Doyle
The Missing Scientist	S.F. Stevens
The Red Badge of Courage	Stephen Crane
Robinson Crusoe	Daniel Defoe
Seven Chinese Stories	T.J. Sheridan
Stories of Shakespeare's Plays 2	Retold by Wyatt & Fullerton
A Tale of Two Cities	Charles Dickens
Tales of Crime and Detection	Retold by G.F. Wear
Two Boxes of Gold and Other Stories	Charles Dickens

Grade 3

Vocabulary restricted to 3700 headwords
Illustrated in colour

Battle of Wits at Crimson Cliff	Retold by Benjamin Chia
Dr Jekyll and Mr Hyde and Other Stories	R.L. Stevenson
From Russia, with Love	Ian Fleming
The Gifts and Other Stories	O. Henry & Others
The Good Earth	Pearl S. Buck
Journey to the Centre of the Earth	Jules Verne
Kidnapped	R.L. Stevenson
King Solomon's Mines	H. Rider Haggard
Lady Precious Stream	S.I. Hsiung
The Light of Day	Eric Ambler
Moonraker	Ian Fleming
The Moonstone	Wilkie Collins
A Night of Terror and Other Strange Tales	Guy De Maupassant
Seven Stories	H.G. Wells
Stories of Shakespeare's Plays 3	Retold by H.G. Wyatt
Tales of Mystery and Imagination	Edgar Allan Poe
20,000 Leagues Under the Sea	Jules Verne
The War of the Worlds	H.G. Wells
The Woman in White	Wilkie Collins
Wuthering Heights	Emily Brontë
You Only Live Twice	Ian Fleming

Grade 4

Vocabulary within a 5000 headwords range
Illustrated in black and white

The Diamond as Big as the Ritz and Other Stories	F. Scott Fitzgerald
Dragon Seed	Pearl S. Buck
Frankenstein	Mary Shelley
The Mayor of Casterbridge	Thomas Hardy
Pride and Prejudice	Jane Austen
The Stalled Ox and Other Stories	Saki
The Thimble and Other Stories	D.H. Lawrence